The Key Word
and other mysteries

The Key Word
and other mysteries

BY ISAAC ASIMOV

Illustrated by ROD BURKE

AN AVON CAMELOT BOOK

AVON BOOKS
A division of
The Hearst Corporation
959 Eighth Avenue
New York, New York 10019

Published by arrangement with Walker and Company.
Library of Congress Catalog Card Number: 77-4597
ISBN: 0-380-43224-2

First Camelot Printing, March, 1979
Third Printing

AVON TRADEMARK REG. U.S. OFF. AND IN
OTHER COUNTRIES, MARCA REGISTRADA, HECHO EN
U.S.A.

Printed in the U.S.A.

ISAAC ASIMOV is a distinguished scientist as well as a prolific writer who has published over 170 books. His instincts and natural curiosity for probing the unknown and his warm understanding of human nature draw millions of readers—young and old—to his writings.

ROD BURKE began drawing when he was a young child and recalls staying up all night on occasion to give his ideas form and expression on paper. He is an avid reader of science fiction and became a fan of Isaac Asimov's with the publication of the author's famed FOUNDATION TRILOGY. A native midwesterner, Mr. Burke lives in northern Illinois.

CONTENTS

The Key Word

and other mysteries

The Key Word

ORDINARILY, Dad keeps his temper pretty well around the house and he never loses it with me—almost never. I like to think it's because I'm a good kid, but he says it's because I'm smart enough to stay out of his way when he's mad.

I sure didn't stay out of his way this time. He swooped down on me, all red in the face, and snatched *The New York Times* right out from under my hand, "What do you think you're *doing*?," he said. "Don't you have any *brains*?"

I just stood there with my pencil in my hand. I wasn't doing *anything*.

I said, "What's the matter, Dad?" I was just plain astonished.

Mom was hurrying over, too. I guess she

wanted to make sure her one and only son wasn't smashed beyond repair.

"What's the matter?" she asked. "What's he done?"

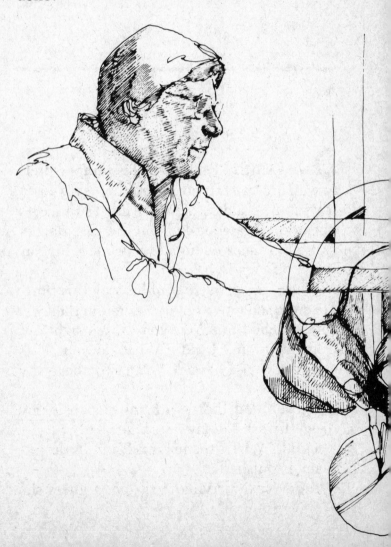

Dad stood there, getting even redder. It was as if he couldn't think what I had done. Then he said, "Doesn't he know better than to touch the paper? That's not our paper."

By that time I sort of got indignant. "Well, how am I supposed to know that, Dad?"

And Mom said, "How *is* he supposed to know? If that's something important, dear, you might have said so. You needn't have left it on the dining room table."

Dad looked as if he wanted to back down, but didn't know how. He said to me, "You didn't tear anything, throw anything away. . . ."

I guess he had become so angry when he saw me at *The Times* that he didn't see what I was doing. "It's in perfect shape," I said.

He walked back and forth in the room, breathing hard, and we just watched him. I figured he must be on a hard case, and when a detective is on a difficult case, you can't blame him for breathing hard.

Then he stopped. He had worked it all out of his system and he was himself again when he turned to me. "I'm sorry, Larry." he said. "I was wrong. It wasn't important. We have the paper micro-filmed anyway. . . . I just can't make anything out of it."

Mom sat down and didn't say anything, because Dad isn't really supposed to talk about his cases at home. I knew that, but I just put a blank look on my face and said, "Out of what, Dad?" And I sat down, too.

Dad looked at us and *he* sat down and threw the paper back on the table. "Out of that. The paper."

I could tell he wanted to talk, so I kept quiet and let him.

After a while, he said, "There's a. . . . Well, never mind what there is, but it's pretty worrisome, and there's a code involved and we can't break it."

"That's not really your job, is it?" Mom asked. "You don't know anything about codes."

"There's something I might do."

I said, "All codes can be broken, can't they?"

"Some not as easy as others, Larry," he said. "Sometimes a code is based on a key word that changes every once in a while, maybe every day. That makes it hard, unless we can find what the key word is, or, better yet, what system they use to change the key word."

"How do you do that?" said Mom.

With a grim look on his face, Dad said, "One way is to pick up somebody's notebook."

"Surely no one would put it in a notebook for people to find," she said.

I butted in. "They would, Mom. You can't

rely on remembering a complicated system, and you can't take chances on forgetting. Right, Dad?"

"Right," he said, "But no one has found a notebook or anything else, and that's it." The tone of his voice told me that was the end of the discussion. "Have you done your homework, Larry?

"All except some of the geography." Then,

to keep from being chased out of the room, I said, "What's *The New York Times* got to do with it?"

That took Dad's mind off the homework. "One of the men we had our eyes on was mugged last night. He managed to fight off the mugger, but he was hurt and we brought him to the hospital. That made it easy to search him very carefully without getting anyone suspicious and scaring them into changing their system or lying low. We got nowhere. No notebook."

"Maybe the mugger got away with . . ." I said.

Dad shook his head. "We had a good man following him. He saw the whole thing. *But* the man being mugged had a *New York Times* on him and he held onto it while he was fighting. I thought that was suspicious, so I had the paper microfilmed and brought it home. I thought there might be some system of picking out one of the words—in a headline on some particular page—last word in some particular column—who knows? Anyone can carry *The Times*. It's not like a notebook. There's nothing suspicious about it."

"How could you tell from the paper what the system was?" I said.

Dad shrugged. "I thought there might be a

mark on it. He might look at the key word and just automatically, without even thinking, check it off. No use. There's not a word in the paper that's marked in any way."

I got excited, "Yes there are!"

Dad gave me that look I always get when he thinks I don't know what I'm talking about. "What do you mean?"

"That's what I was doing when you yelled and grabbed the paper," I said, showing him the pencil I was still holding. "I was doing the crossword puzzle. Don't you see, Dad, it was partly worked out. That's why I started on it, to finish it up."

Dad rubbed his nose. "We noticed that, but what makes you think that has any meaning. Lots of people work on crossword puzzles. It's natural enough."

"Sure, that's why it's a safe system. This one was worked out in the middle, Dad, just a little patch in the middle. No one just does a part in the middle. They start at the upper left corner, with number one."

"If it's a hard puzzle, you might not get a start till you reach the middle."

"It was an easy puzzle, Dad. One across was a three-letter word meaning 'presidential nickname' and that's got to be Ike or Abe, and one down. . . . Anyway, this guy just went straight to that part and didn't bother with anything else. Twenty-seven across was one of the words he worked out and the paper is for yesterday, which is the twenty-seventh of the month."

Dad waited a long while before answering. Then he said, "Coincidence."

"Maybe not," I said. *The Times* crossword puzzle always has at least sixty numbers every day, twice as many on Sunday. Every day of the month has a number and for that day, the key word is the one in that number in the crossword puzzle. If there are two words, across and down, maybe you always take the across."

"Hmm," said Dad.

"How much simpler can it be? Anyone can remember that, and all you have to do is be able to work out crossword puzzles. You can get all kinds of words, long or short, even phrases, even foreign words."

Mom said, "What if a crossword puzzle happens to be too hard to work out just in the crucial spot?"

Now Dad got excited, "They could use each day's puzzle for the day after, and check with the solution to make sure." He had his coat on. ". . . except Sunday, for which the solution comes the next Sunday. . . . I hope

the pencil you used made a different mark
from his, Larry."

"He used a pen," I said.

. . . That wasn't all there was to the case,
but they did break the code. Dad got a bonus
and he put it in the bank toward my college
education.

He said it was only fair.

Santa Claus
Gets a Coin

DAD doesn't usually bring his work home
with him, but it was the Christmas season,
December 22, and it was just spoiling every-
thing. There's nothing like an unsolved problem to keep a detective from concentrating
on enjoying a holiday.

It was a little thing, not a murder or a
bombing or anything big, but it's the little
things that can get under your skin.

"Can you imagine," he said that evening,
"picking up one of those coins in a Santa
Claus bucket? It was a youngster who threw it
in, too."

We knew what he meant. The newspapers
called it "the Christmas coin mystery." The
museum began to miss valuable coins just as
the Christmas season started. It seemed like

an inside job, but that meant a hundred people at least and there were no leads.

"A youngster?" I said.

"A kid about your age, Larry, and he goes to your junior high," Dad said. "He dropped one of those coins in a bucket with one of those Santa Claus's ringing his bell over it. The Santa Claus saw it wasn't an American coin and since he had his stand near the museum, he thought it might be one of the stolen ones. Being honest, he turned it in. He could identify the kid, too. It was a neigh-

borhood kid and he'd seen him often. A shame. Christmas, too."

Mom looked very upset. "You mean the *child* was the thief."

"No," said Dad. "But, you know, he had to

be questioned and that upset his parents. It spoiled their Christmas, I'm sure."

"What happened, Dad?" I asked. "Where did the kid get the coin?"

"A man inside the museum gave it to him and asked him to drop it in the Santa Claus. He gave him a quarter to do it."

"Can the kid identify the man who gave him the coin?"

"No," said my father, shaking his head. "He didn't really look. You know how kids are."

That annoyed me a little. I said, "No, Dad, I don't know how kids are."

Dad cleared his throat. "It was the fifth coin that had been taken and the museum has been tightening its security. We don't know what system the thief used to dispose of the coins once he had them, but it must have been getting harder for him to do so. This time he must have sensed that he'd be caught if he left the museum with it on him, so he got the kid to take it out for him."

"And put it in the Santa Claus bucket?" I said. "That was stupid."

Dad shrugged. "He was in a hurry, maybe. It might have been the first place that occurred to him. Maybe he thought he could get it back later."

For a while after that I just ate my dessert (we had baked apple) and thought hard. Then I went to the dictionary for a minute or two. When I came back I said, "Dad, is there a crèche near where the Santa Claus was standing? You know, a set of little statues of the stable at Bethlehem and the infant Jesus and the Virgin and Joseph and cows and donkeys."

"I know what a crèche is," he said, "so don't go pretending you have to educate me. The answer is No."

That was disappointing because I had hoped I would show up as a great detective. But then Mom said, "There's one to the south of the museum, just outside one of the churches. I see it when I'm shopping."

"How near the museum, Mom?"

"Less than a block away from the southern edge," she said.

"The Santa Claus got his coin near the northern edge," Dad said.

"Could I speak to the kid myself, Dad? He might not mind talking to another kid and I'd like to ask him something."

Dad said, "Like to ask him *what*, Larry?"

But I shook my head. "You know how kids are, Dad. I just want to check it out, first."

"All right, then." I guess he was a little

embarrassed at having sneered at kids, so he gave in. "But you go easy, son," he said. "Don't make it hard on the boy."

It was dark when we got there and it looked like a sort of dinky apartment. The man who opened the door seemed unhappy when he saw Dad. "Is something else wrong?" he asked in a worried voice.

"No," said Dad, "but my son wants to talk to yours if he's home."

He was, and I recognized him and even knew his name. He wasn't a friend of mine exactly, but I had seen him around the halls at school. He was a class lower than I was.

We went to one side to be private, and I said, "Tom, did that man say to drop the coin in the Santa Claus?"

"Yes, he did."

"Didn't he say 'drop it in Santa Claus's bucket.'?"

"No. He said, 'in the Santa Claus.' I remember because I thought maybe I should drop the coin in the Santa Claus's mouth but I guess he meant the bucket."

"Maybe he said something that *sounded* like Santa Claus. Was it *exactly* Santa Claus?"

Tom looked confused. Then he smiled and said, "Oh, he didn't say Santa Claus. He said

Kriss Kringle, but that's the same thing, isn't it?"

I could have shouted and jumped up and down, but I managed to play it cool. "It's another name for Santa Claus," I admitted, "but it's a different word. So he asked you to drop the coin in the Kriss Kringle. Not in Kriss Kringle's bucket, but in the Kriss Kringle?"

"Yes. He asked me if I knew where that was, and I said sure, and ran off. Heck, I saw that Santa Claus ringing his bell every day for a couple of weeks now."

"Thanks, Tom," I said.

Dad looked plenty puzzled, but I wouldn't say a word till we found the crèche that Mom had mentioned. I could still be all wrong.

But once we got there, there was no doubt. The crèche had lights on it and there was a little slit near the infant Jesus and over it was a sign that said, 'For the Poor this Holiday Season.'

"There, Dad," I pointed at the spot. "The coins are in there, if it hasn't been opened yet."

Dad got the sexton of the church and he opened up the poor box. There were coins and bills in it and also the four coins from the

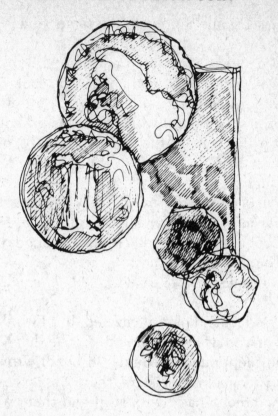

museum. They were going to open it on Christmas Day, you see, and I guess the thief knew that.

"You know, Dad," I said afterward, "I *thought* it didn't make sense to say 'in the Santa Claus' and I tried to think of what else the man might have said that could have been taken for Santa Claus. I couldn't think of anything but Kriss Kringle. I looked that up in the dictionary and it comes from 'Christkindl' which in German is pronounced almost like Kriss Kringle. It means 'little Christ child' and I suppose there were legends that the Christ child brought presents on Christmas so the word came to mean Santa Claus. That crèche was a good place to hide the coins if you knew it wasn't going to be opened till Christmas. I'll bet the thief planned to break it open the night before. I hope he wasn't planning to take the rest of the money, too. That would be *really* mean."

Dad said, "Good thinking, Larry. It doesn't help us get the man, but at least we have the coins back."

"Sure it helps you get the man, Dad. It's someone who was so excited, he forgot to tell Tom to put the coin in the *Christchild* but said it in German and told him to put it in the *Christkindl* so that Tom thought he meant Kriss Kringle. All you have to do is get someone in the museum who speaks German better than he speaks English. That ought to cut it down a lot."

It did. They had the thief before Christmas Day and the museum gave Tom a hundred-dollar reward for remembering the word and a hundred dollars to the Santa Claus for turning the coin in. That made it a good Christmas for both of them.

I wouldn't take a reward because I was just doing my job as detective, but it made it a good Christmas for me, too.

Sarah Tops

I CAME OUT of the Museum of Natural History and was crossing the street on my way to the subway, when I saw the crowd about halfway down the block; and the police cars, too. I could hear the whine of an approaching ambulance.

For a minute I hesitated, but then I walked on. The crowds of the curious just get in the way of officials trying to save lives. My Dad, who's a detective on the force, complains about that all the time, and I wasn't going to add to the difficulty myself.

I just kept my mind on the term paper I was going to have to write on air-pollution for my 7th-grade class and mentally arranged the notes I had taken on the Museum program on the subject.

Of course, I knew I would read about it in the afternoon papers. Besides, I would ask Dad about it after dinner. Sometimes he talked about cases without giving too much of the real security details. And Mom and I never talk about what we hear, anyway.

After I asked, Mom looked kind of funny and said, "He was in the museum at the very time."

I said, "I was working on my term paper. I was there first thing in the morning."

Mom looked worried. "There might have been shooting in the museum."

"Well, there wasn't," said Dad soothingly. "This man tried to lose himself in the museum and he didn't succeed."

"I would have," I said. "I know the museum, every inch."

Dad doesn't like me boasting, so he frowned at me. "The thugs who were after him didn't let him get away entirely. They caught up with him outside, knifed him, and got away. We'll catch them, though. We know who they are.

He nodded his head. "They're what's left of the gang that broke into that jewelry store two weeks ago. We managed to get the jewels back, but we didn't grab all the men. And not all the jewels either. One diamond was left. A

big one—worth thirty thousand dollars."

"Maybe that's what the killers were after," I said.

"Very likely. The dead man was probably trying to cross the other two and get off with that one stone for himself. They turned out his pockets, practically ripped off his clothes, after they knifed him."

"Did they get the diamond?" I asked.

"How can we tell? The woman who reported the killing came on him when he was just barely able to breathe. She said he said three words to her, very slowly, 'Try . . . Sarah . . . Tops.' Then he died."

"Who is Sarah Tops?" asked Mom.

Dad shrugged. "I don't know. I don't even know if that's really what he said. The woman was pretty hysterical. If she's right and that's what he said, then maybe the killers didn't get the diamond. Maybe the dead man left it with Sarah Tops, whoever she is. Maybe he knew he was dying and wanted to give it back and have it off his conscience."

"Is there a Sarah Tops in the phone book, Dad?" I asked.

Dad said, "Did you think we didn't look? No Sarah Tops, either one P or two P's. Nothing in the city directory. Nothing in our files. Nothing in the FBI files."

Mom said, "Maybe it's not a person. Maybe it's a firm. Sarah Tops Cakes or something."

"Could be," said Dad. "There's no Sarah Tops firm, but there are other kinds of Tops and they'll be checked out for anyone working there named Sarah. It'll take days of dull routine."

I got an idea suddenly and bubbled over. "Listen, Dad, maybe it isn't a firm either. Maybe it's a *thing*. Maybe the woman didn't hear 'Sarah Tops' but 'Sarah's top'; you know, a *top* that you spin. If the dead guy has a daughter named Sarah, maybe he gouged a bit out of her top and stashed the diamond inside and . . ."

Dad pointed his finger at me and grinned, "Very good, Larry," he said, "A nice idea. But he doesn't have a daughter named Sarah. Or any relative by that name as far as we know. We've searched where he lived and there's nothing reported there that can be called a top."

"Well," I said, sort of let down and disappointed, "I suppose that's not such a good idea anyway, because why should he say we ought to *try* it? He either hid it in Sarah's top or he didn't. He would know which. Why should he say we should *try* it?"

And then it hit me. What if. . . .

Dad was just getting up, as if he were going to turn on television, and I said, "Dad, can you get into the museum this time of evening?"

"On police business? Sure."

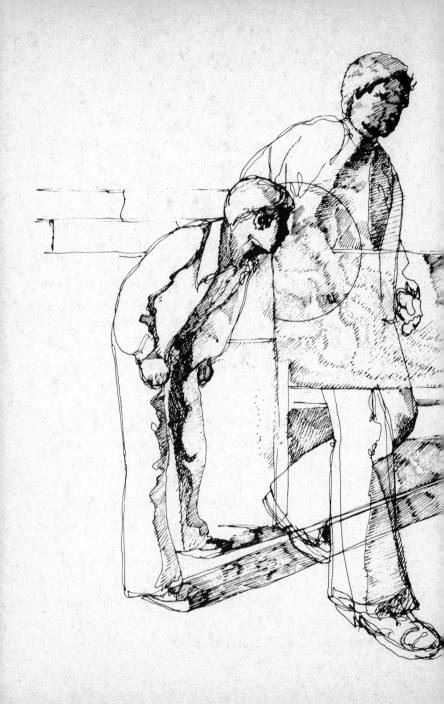

"Dad," I said, kind of breathless, "I think we better go look. *Now*. Before the people start coming in again."

"Why?"

"I've got a silly idea. I . . . I . . ."

Dad didn't push me. He likes me to have my own ideas. He thinks maybe I'll be a detective, too, some day. He said, "All right. Let's follow up your lead whatever it is."

He called the museum, then we took a taxi and got there just when the last purple bit of twilight was turning to black. We were let in by a guard.

I'd never been in the museum when it was dark. It looked like a huge, underground cave, with the guard's flashlight seeming to make things even darker and more mysterious.

We took the elevator up to the fourth floor where the big shapes loomed in the bit of light that shone this way and that as the guard moved his flash.

"Do you want me to put on the light in this room?" he asked.

"Yes, please," I said.

There they all were. Some in glass cases; but the big ones in the middle of the large room. Bones and teeth and spines of giants that ruled the earth hundreds of millions of years ago.

"I want to look close at that one," I said. "Is it all right if I climb over the railing?"

"Go ahead," said the guard. He helped me.

I leaned against the platform, looking at the grayish plaster material the skeleton was standing on.

"What's this?" I said. It didn't look much different in color from the plaster on which it was lying.

"Chewing gum," said the guard, frowning. "Those darn kids . . ."

"The guy was trying to get away and he saw his chance to throw this . . . keep it away from *them*. . . ." Before I could finish my sentence Dad took the gum from me. He squeezed it, then pulled it apart. Something inside caught the light and flashed. Dad put it in an envelope. "How did you know?" he asked me.

"Well, look at it," I said.

It was a magnificent skeleton. It had a large skull with bone stretching back over the neck vertebrae. It had two horns over the eyes, and a third one, just a bump, on the snout. The nameplate said *Triceratops*.

The Thirteenth
Day of Christmas

THIS WAS one year we were *glad* when Christmas Day was over.

It had been a grim Christmas Eve and I had stayed awake as long as I could, half listening for bombs. And Mom and I stayed up until midnight on Christmas *Day*, too. Then Dad called and said, "Okay, it's over. Nothing's happened. I'll be home as soon as I can."

Mom and I danced around as if Santa Claus had just come and then, after about an hour, Dad came home and I went to bed and slept fine.

You see, it's special in our house. Dad's a detective on the force and these days, with terrorists and bombings, it can get pretty hairy. So, when on December 20th, warnings reached headquarters that there would be a Christmas Day bombing at the Soviet offices in the United Nations, it had to be taken seriously.

The entire force was put on the alert and the FBI came in, too. The Soviets had their own security, I guess, but none of it satisfied Dad.

The day before Christmas was the worst. "If someone is crazy enough to want to plant a bomb and if he's not too worried about getting caught afterward, he's likely to be able to do it no matter what precautions we take." Dad's voice had a grimness we rarely heard.

"I suppose there's no way of knowing who it is," Mom said.

Dad shook his head. "Letters from newspapers pasted on paper; no fingerprints; only smudges. Common stuff we can't trace and a threat that it would be the only warning we'd get. What can we do?"

"Well, it must be someone who doesn't like the Russians, I guess," Mom said.

Dad said, "That doesn't narrow it much. Of course, the Soviets say it's a Zionist threat, and we've got to keep an eye on the Jewish Defense League."

"Gee, Dad," I said. "That doesn't make much sense. The Jewish people wouldn't pick Christmas to do it, would they? It doesn't mean anything to them; and it doesn't

mean anything to the Soviet Union, either. They're officially atheistic."

"You can't reason that out to the Russians," Dad said. "Now why don't you turn in, because tomorrow may be a bad day all round, Christmas or not."

Then he left. He was out all Christmas, and it was pretty rotten. We didn't even open any presents; just sat listening to the radio which was tuned to the news station.

Then at midnight when Dad called and nothing had happened, we could breathe again, but I still forgot to open my presents.

That didn't come till the morning of the 26th. We made *that* day Christmas. Dad had a day off and Mom baked the turkey a day late. It wasn't till after dinner that we talked about it at all.

Mom said, "I suppose the person, whoever it was, couldn't find any way of planting the bomb once the Department drew the security strings tight."

Dad smiled, as if he appreciated Mom's loyalty. "I don't think you can make security that tight," he said, "but what's the difference? There was no bomb. Maybe it was a bluff. After all, it did disrupt the city a bit and it gave the Soviet people at the United Nations some sleepless nights, I'll bet. That might have been almost as good for the bomber as letting the bomb go off."

"If he couldn't do it on Christmas," I said, "maybe he'll do it another time. Maybe he just said Christmas to get everyone keyed up and then, after they relax, he'll. . . ."

Dad gave me one of his little pushes on the side of my head. "You're a cheerful one, Larry. . . . No, I don't think so. Real bombers value the sense of power. When they say something is going up at a certain time, it's got to be that time or it's no fun for them."

I was still suspicious, but the days passed and there was no bombing and the Department gradually went back to normal. The

FBI left and even the Soviet people seemed to forget about it, according to Dad.

On January 2, the Christmas-New Years vacation was over and I went back to school. We started rehearsing our Christmas pageant. We didn't call it that, of course, because we're not supposed to have religious celebrations at school, what with the separation of church and state. We just made an elaborate show out of the song, "The Twelve Days of Christmas," which doesn't have any religion to it—just presents.

There were twelve of us kids, each one singing a particular line every time it came up and then coming in all together on the partridge in a pear tree. I was number five, singing 'five gold rings' because I was still a boy soprano and I could hit that high note pretty nicely, if I do say so myself.

Some kids didn't know why Christmas had twelve days, but I explained that if we count Christmas Day as one, the twelfth day after is January 6, when the Three Wise Men arrived with gifts for the Christ child. Naturally, it was on January 6, that we put on the show in the auditorium, with as many parents there as wanted to come.

Dad got a few hours off and was sitting in

the audience with Mom. I could see him getting set to hear his son's high note for the last time because next year my voice changes or I know the reason why.

Did you ever get an idea in the middle of a stage show and have to continue, no matter what?

We were only on the second day with its 'two turtle-doves' when I thought, "Oh my, it's the *thirteenth* day of Christmas." The whole world was shaking about me and I couldn't do a thing but stay on the stage and sing about five gold rings.

I didn't think they'd ever get to those stupid 'twelve drummers drumming.' It was like having itching powder on instead of underwear. I couldn't stand still. Then, when the last note was out, while they were still applauding, I broke away, went jumping down the steps from the platform and up the aisle calling, "Dad!"

He looked startled, but I grabbed him, and I think I was babbling so fast, he could hardly understand.

I said, "Dad, Christmas isn't the same day everywhere. It could be one of the Soviet's own people. They're officially atheist, but maybe one of them is religious and he wants to place the bomb for that reason. Only he would be a member of the Russian Orthodox Church. They don't go by our calendar."

"What," said Dad, looking as if he didn't understand a word I was saying.

"It's *so*, Dad. I read about it. The Russian Orthodox Church is still on the Julian Calendar, which the west gave up for the Gregorian

Calendar centuries ago. The Julian Calendar is thirteen days behind ours. The Orthodox Christmas is on *their* December 25, which is *our* January 7. It's *tomorrow*.

He didn't believe me, just like that. He looked it up in the almanac; then he called up someone in the Department who was Russian Orthodox.

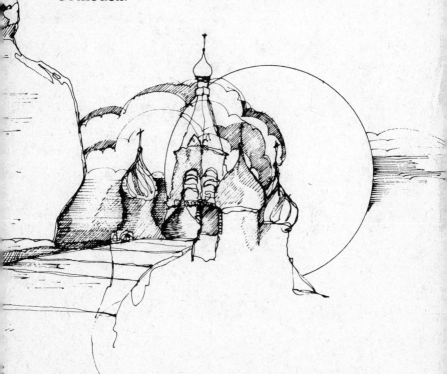

He was able to get the Department moving again. They talked to the Soviets, and once the Soviets stopped talking about Zionists and looked at themselves, they got the man. I don't know what they did with him, but there was no bombing on the thirteenth day of Christmas, either.

The Department wanted to give me a new bicycle for Christmas after that, but I turned it down. I was just doing my duty.

A Case of Need

THE THING about Jimmy Franklin is that he *needed* those questions. Everyone agreed that was why he had to look at them on the sly.

He was the only kid in my junior high who wasn't watching the big Nostalgia Contest, because he was way behind and his father was sore at him. So he asked to be allowed to study in his homeroom instead. That was just across the hall from the science room, and that looked bad for him, too.

But that's not the way it looked to me. Jimmy didn't need those questions to get ahead as badly as someone else might need them to *stay* ahead.

I'm sort of inbetween myself. I don't mind high marks, but I'm philosophic about not getting them sometimes. My Dad is a detec-

tive on the police force and someday I'm
going to be one and I figure you need a different kind of smart for that than being a school
whiz-kid. Dad says you need all kinds of
smart, though, and sometimes I think he's
right.

Anyway, the Nostalgia Contest wasn't my
thing, and I let it go. It had been set up by
some businessmen, who got advertising out
of it, I suppose, and the parents seemed to
think it was a good idea. I mean, it was nostalgia for *them*.

The kids had to answer questions about the
1930's. That's ancient history to us, but parents had a better chance to know and that
made them feel smarter than the kids—for
once.

I might have done all right, but I didn't
think I should take all that time away from my
regular studies. I'd have had to do a lot of
reading. Besides, I figured Nancy Gilroy
would win. She'd won every contest she en-
tered, just about—spelling bees, current
events, and so on. It was very important to
her.

And that's the thing. Nancy had to do a lot
of studying for the contest and she must have
gotten scared that she'd do badly on the science finals. She *had* to see those questions.

Old man Randolph, who teaches science, might just have changed the questions when he found the papers disturbed, but he's a mean man. He gave the test anyway and when Jimmy Franklin did pretty well, he accused him in front of everybody.

Jimmy said he had studied hard, but no one believed him. He had been right across the hall. Everyone else was in the auditorium. It had to be him—except I didn't think so. I was a good friend of Jimmy's and he wasn't the sort of kid to do it. I suspected Nancy.

So it was a problem. I wasn't exactly keen on getting someone into trouble, but didn't I have to get someone *out* of a trouble he didn't deserve?

I put it to Dad.

He didn't ask for details. He realized it was my problem. He just said, "Leaving a crime unsolved means that innocent people may carry the burden of suspicion all their lives. If the only way to prove their innocence is to point out the guilty one, shouldn't that be done?"

I said, "Maybe the guilty person will confess rather than let it be pinned on the innocent one."

Dad smiled with only half his mouth.

"Don't count on it," he said.

So I knew what I had to do.

I had been in the auditorium, of course. Everyone was. Nancy Gilroy was in the final round—she and five other kids—and they were down to real small things. I could have answered most of them because I like history, but I could never do it under pressure. I'd have stood there stuttering if the whole school had been watching. It never seemed to bother Nancy. Realizing that was what had started me thinking.

The first time she was up, the question was this: "What do the initials HST, HAW, and JNG have in common, and what do they stand for?

Right away I know that HST had to be Harry S. Truman. That meant that the other two sets of initials had to be. . . .

But Nancy got it out before I could even think it. In that funny high-pitched voice of hers she said, "Those are the initials of the three Vice-Presidents who served under President Franklin Delano Roosevelt."

She was right, of course. Then she had to name each one in the order they had given. HST was Harry S. Truman and she explained that the S didn't stand for anything. HAW was

Henry Agard Wallace, and JNG—but that's where she broke down.

She said, "John Garner," in a sort of whisper and when the quizmaster said, "What's the middle name?" she just stared, shook her head and dashed off the stage crying.

Some of the kids laughed, but mostly they were sorry and embarrassed. Maybe I was the only one who was puzzled. Later on, after the contest was nearly over, she was sitting in the last row, her face all red and puffy.

Later, when the fuss about the questions

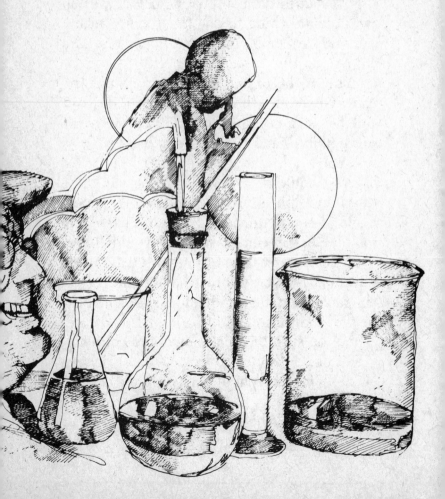

came up, I figured she had gone out to look at the questions after she had run from the stage—just so she could stay first in science.

And she did stay first. She handed in a perfect paper, but of course, no one was surprised at that.

So I had to go to the principal. It was an awfully hard thing to do. He frowned at me and said, "Are you saying that James Franklin did *not* do this thing."

"No, sir, he didn't," I said, "He's not the kind. Of course, there's no proof he did, sir, and he isn't being expelled, but everyone suspects him and that's just as bad."

"I can't help that," the principal said. "No one else could have done it, unless you think Mr. Randolph is mistaken about his papers having been disturbed. That's not likely. He took special precautions and he wouldn't lie."

So I had to explain I thought it was Nancy Gilroy and that she must have done it after she ran off the stage and before she came back to the auditorium. "If you ask her," I said, "she'll be sure to break down and confess."

He said, "Nancy Gilroy is the brightest student in the school. Why should she do such a thing?"

I said, "Maybe to stay the brightest, sir. She got into the Nostalgia Contest and it turned out to be too much and she was losing out on her regular work. She finally decided the science finals were more important than the contest, so she deliberately muffed that question so she could. . . ."

"I can't believe this, young man," he said in a hard voice. "You have no evidence and no right to make such accusations."

I felt hot all over, but I couldn't back down. "I have better evidence against Nancy than anyone has against Jimmy," I said. "It was a bad break for Nancy to be asked that particular question, because it was impossible for her to muff it the way she did. She was under a strain and didn't think fast enough."

"And how can you tell she couldn't miss the answer? Are you a mind reader?"

"No, sir, but I knew the answer to that question and I looked it up to make sure. Nancy knew that Harry Truman's middle name was just an S. She knew that Henry Wallace's middle name was Agard, and that's where she *should* have muffed it, because she couldn't possibly forget John Garner's middle name the way she pretended."

"*I* don't remember Garner's middle name," said the principal. "It isn't strange for Nancy not to."

It was my answer to that that got the principal to question Nancy and, of course, she *did* confess.

I said, "How could Nancy forget her own name. sir? John Garner's middle name was Nance."

Winner of the Newbery Medal

THE SUMMER OF THE SWANS

by Betsy Byars

illustrated by Ted CoConis

What had changed in Sara she did not know. Her moods were as unaccountable as the sudden appearance of the swans which so fascinated Charlie, her mentally retarded younger brother, as he watched them glide silently across the lake.

Suddenly, one night, Charlie disappeared—and Sara's own miseries were left behind as she searched for Charlie, who wandered somewhere, lost, helpless, and bewildered. Sara turned to Joe Melby, and together they found him. The longest day of the summer was over, and Sara knew she would never be quite the same.

An Avon Camelot Book
46961 $1.50

Also by Betsy Byars
AFTER THE GOAT MAN   41590 $1.25
THE MIDNIGHT FOX   46987 $1.50
RAMA THE GYPSY CAT   41608 $1.25
TROUBLE RIVER   47001 $1.50
THE WINGED COLT OF CASA MIA   46995 $1.50

An old mansion, a graveyard, and a mysterious skull!

UNCLE ROBERT'S SECRET

by Wylly Folk St. John

"You don't know what scared is till you've fallen out of a tree late at night into a bunch of broken-down gravestones, practically on top of somebody you think might be a mean guy ... and there's an awful scream still ringing in your ears."

Bob should have known how hard it would be to keep a secret, especially when that secret happened to be a bedraggled little boy named Tim. And when Bob finally shared it with his brother and sister, they suddenly found themselves involved in a very spooky mystery.

An Avon Camelot Book
46326 $1.50

Gilly Ground was an orphan and all he wanted was a little peace and quiet . . .

DORP DEAD

by Julia Cunningham

illustrated by James Spanfeller

Life in the orphanage was difficult in many ways. Gilly spent as much time as he could in the abandoned tower in the woods. It was peaceful there—and it was there that Gilly met the Hunter. Then, one day, he was placed in a foster home. And Gilly felt as though he were trapped in a nightmare come true.

An Avon Camelot Book
29876 $1.25

Also by Julia Cunningham
DEAR RAT   46615 $1.50

A suspenseful mystery with a surprise ending!

THE CHRISTMAS TREE MYSTERY

by Wylly Folk St. John

Beth Carlton was in trouble. She accused Pete Abel of steal-
ing the Christmas ornaments from her family tree, something
she knew he hadn't done. And what was worse—the police
believed her! Beth had two days to prove to the police that
Pete wasn't a thief, and all she had to go on was her step-
brother's word that Pete was innocent.

An Avon Camelot Book
46300 $1.50